The Stinking Story
of
GARBAGE

Katie Daynes

Illustrated by Uwe Mayer

Garbage consultant: Alan Munson
Recycling Manager at Viridor Waste Management

Reading consultant: Alison Kelly
Roehampton University

Contents

Chapter 1

In the beginning

Long, long ago, there was no
garbage on Earth. There were no
living things either. Gradually,
plants and animals developed and
created their own natural waste.

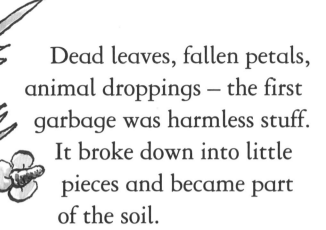

Dead leaves, fallen petals,
animal droppings – the first
garbage was harmless stuff.
It broke down into little
pieces and became part
of the soil.

Then came humans. To begin
with, their waste was harmless too.

The first humans were always on the move, hunting animals and gathering berries. All they left behind them were ash, feces, bones and rotten fruit.

When humans decided to settle and farm the land, their garbage became useful. They fed leftover fruit and vegetables to their animals... and dung made excellent fertilizer for the fields.

Over time, humans thought up
new objects for everyday life.

They dried
animal skins to
use as clothes...

made tools by
fitting sharp
stones to sticks...

...and shaped
and baked clay
soil to make
jugs and bowls.

Every item was treasured and looked after. Only once it was beyond repair would someone finally throw it away.

Chapter 2

Piling up

Around a thousand years ago,
small towns were appearing all
over Europe. Lots of people in one
place meant lots of garbage too.

Dry garbage could be burned on fires at home, but there was no way to cope with sludgy waste.

The town dwellers frowned. "In the country, people bury what the pigs don't eat. But here we have no pigs... and nowhere to dig."

Soon, food and toilet waste piled up in the streets, smelling awful and attracting rats and diseases. This didn't stop people from moving in from the countryside.

Traders knew there was money to be made in towns. They set up shops next to each other and dumped their garbage in the street.

Locals named the streets after the shops. One street of butcher shops in London was called "Stinking Lane" because of the stench of rotting meat outside.

With no drains, toilet waste was a stinky problem. People learned to fear the cry, "Gardy loo!" It meant the contents of someone's toilet pot were about to be emptied from a window...

Gardy loo!

...onto the street below.

"Gardy loo" came from the French for "watch out for the water" – but this water was yellow and horribly smelly. Polite gentlemen in Paris let ladies walk closer to the road, where they were less likely to get splattered.

In 1297, a British law ordered everyone to keep their front door clear of garbage. So they did. They dumped their waste outside someone else's house instead.

Streets became smellier and the rats multiplied, feasting on garbage and spreading diseases.

In the 1330s, a vicious plague broke out in Constantinople and spread across Europe. The "Black Death" reached England in 1347 and killed two thirds of the people in London.

Rats caught the plague first. Their fleas jumped onto passing humans... and gave them the plague too. But all people knew at the time was that rats and garbage meant trouble.

"Rakers" were employed to rake up garbage in London. It was either sold as compost or dumped in marshlands. In Germany, farmers delivering food to cities had to fill their carts with garbage for the journey home.

But dumping garbage outside cities created other problems. When King Edward III took a ride along the riverbank in London, he was appalled to see smelly garbage floating past.

This shouldn't be allowed!

After his death, there was a new British law. It banned people from throwing garbage into ditches or rivers.

Eventually, drains were introduced, followed by flushing toilets. These weren't new ideas. The oldest drainpipe, found in Iraq, dates back 6,000 years.

The royal family in Crete had flushing toilets 3,000 years ago.

And 2,000 years ago, an underground drain was built in Rome so vast someone could row a boat down it.

But somehow these ideas had been forgotten. Only when human waste was overflowing did people invent drains and toilets again.

Sir John Harington's flush toilet

Chapter 3

Industrial waste

In the 1800s, new inventions led to new businesses. They transformed the way people lived in Europe and America – and multiplied the amount of garbage they produced.

Steam engines were designed, machines were built and factories were set up. They churned out thousands of objects a day, creating lots of waste along the way.

Each factory needed hundreds of workers. People flooded in from the countryside, hoping to find new jobs in town.

Towns just couldn't grow fast enough and the garbage piled higher. Even worse, with factories making new products to buy, people owned more things to throw away.

Scavengers earned a living from sifting through the garbage. They sold discarded wood and coal as fuel, turned old rags into new clothes and boiled up bones to make glue.

21

Even dog mess had a price. Leather makers bought it to clean their animal skins.

For richer pickings, the search went underground. Many precious items were lost down the drains, but only desperate scavengers risked the sewers to find them.

In the 1830s and 1840s, cholera epidemics threatened the lives of thousands in Asia and Europe. Cholera is a dangerous disease caused by dirty food or water. When governments realized that garbage was to blame, they quickly announced new health laws.

"Each town must keep its streets clean," declared the politicians.

"We'll dig giant pits in the countryside," they continued, "and bury all our garbage there."

These pits were soon known as landfill sites.

At last garbage had an official place to go. But raking it up and loading it onto carts was a yucky business.

In 1875, the British government had another brainwave. "Let's design something for people to put their garbage *in*," they thought. "Then collect it from them once a week."

Ash bin

Fred

Pillar pot

Waste bucket

Trash can

Ye garbage can design competition

Eight years later, a city official in Paris, Eugène Poubelle, had a similar idea. He ordered landlords to provide containers for garbage and organized a weekly collection.

Reluctantly, the landlords obeyed. They named the containers "poubelles" after the bossy Eugène. French garbage cans are still called "poubelles" today.

Meanwhile, America had its own worries. In 1842, a report left Americans in no doubt – dirty conditions led to deadly diseases. They had to clean up their towns, fast. But where could all the garbage go?

The great garbage plan

Burn it?

Ignore it?

Garbage

Bury it?

Eat it?

In 1885, America's first incinerator was built. It was a huge building with a fiery furnace. In a flash, it reduced vast amounts of garbage to ashes...

and spewed out horrible smoke.

Before long, hundreds more incinerators were being built.

Sending cart loads of city garbage to be eaten by pigs also seemed like a good idea.

But one by one, the pigs became sick and had to be killed.

In the 1920s, landfill sites reached America. Instead of digging pits, some Americans decided to dump their garbage in swamps. It took much less effort and a swamp filled with garbage could then be sold as dry land.

Chapter 4

Garbage collection

Until the 1920s, garbage was taken away by horse and cart. Then gasoline-powered trucks were invented.

At first, trucks were just horseless carts.

Later, roofs were added, trapping garbage and its smell inside.

After that, the trucks were made lower, so they were easier to load, and "packer blades" were introduced. These scooped the garbage into the truck and squashed it to make room for more.

Garbage inside truck

Packer blade

Today, garbage trucks even have robot arms to pick up and empty garbage cans.

In large towns, garbage trucks unload at a transfer station.

The contents of four trucks scrunch up into one box.

Then the boxes travel to a landfill or incinerator by truck, train or ship.

Some trucks have different compartments inside. When they stop outside a house, someone jumps out and sorts glass, metal, plastic and paper garbage into four separate sections.

Chapter 5

Plastic problems

Thanks to garbage cans and trash collectors, our streets are now much cleaner. But getting rid of garbage altogether is becoming harder.

In the 1950s, an exciting new product changed garbage forever – plastic. The Americans first invented plastic in 1862. They developed and improved it until they could mold it into any shape.

Before long, furniture, TVs, toilet seats and diapers were being made from plastic. And everything from razor blades to frozen peas was being packaged in it.

Today, people buy more products than ever. They rip off the packaging and throw it away.

Every minute, one million plastic bags are handed out across the world. Most of them are used once then left in a trash can.

In just one year, a baby can go through 1,800 plastic diapers.

The amount of garbage is not the only problem. It takes 500 years for plastic to break down and dissolve into the ground. That means every plastic bag and dirty diaper ever dumped in a landfill is still sitting there.

Chapter 6
What a waste

While most people are trying to bury garbage, some people are digging for it. Archaeologists examine garbage from the past to find out how people used to live...

Take my brooch when you go to war.

Thank you, my darling.

They've even developed tests to show how old the garbage is. Whether it's a rusty iron dagger, a broken brooch or the remains of someone's dinner, each item provides a clue to life long ago.

But no one's interested in modern garbage. They just want to get rid of it.

Today, there are twice as many people in the world as there were 100 years ago. And they're making more garbage than ever. An average person throws away four times their body weight in a year.

In one day, American businesses create enough paperwork to circle the Earth 20 times.

In three months, Americans throw away enough aluminum to rebuild all their passenger planes.

And if all the steel cans used in Britain and Ireland each year were placed end to end, they would reach to the Moon and back...

...three times.

Dealing with all this garbage is big business. Many companies make money by offering garbage clearing services.

They may clean the streets at the end of the day...

or shred secret business documents.

Most garbage is taken to landfill sites or incinerators. But the story doesn't end there...

Over the years, garbage in landfills breaks down, producing disgusting liquids and the gases methane and carbon dioxide.

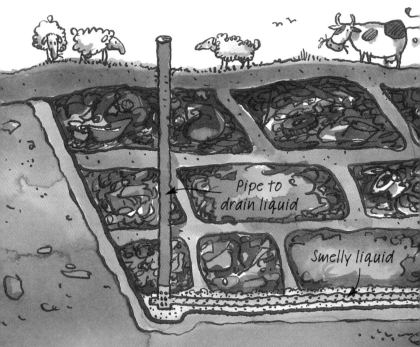

Pipe to drain liquid

Smelly liquid

Landfill workers line the earth with strong, protective material, to stop any leaks. They also collect the methane so it doesn't explode.

When a landfill is full, workers carefully cover it and plant it with grass. The methane can be used to make electricity.

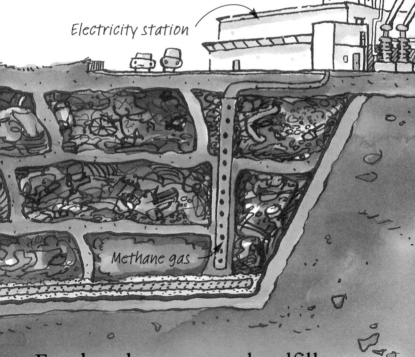

Electricity station

Methane gas

For decades to come, landfill companies must monitor their old sites. They make sure the land is safe and that there are no leaks.

Incinerators aren't a simple story either. Burning garbage may save space, but it gives off harmful gases which have to be treated. And there are mountains of ash to deal with too...

People campaigning for a cleaner world have come up with three suggestions. They call them the "three Rs."

1. **R**EDUCE THE AMOUNT YOU THROW AWAY.

2. **R**EUSE THE THINGS YOU OWN.

3. **R**ECYCLE WHAT YOU CAN.

Chapter 7

Useful garbage

Lots of things people throw away aren't really garbage at all. Books, toys, clothes and shoes can be taken to charity shops and sold again.

Many items are easily repaired by a dab of glue or a needle and thread.

Food and garden waste can be turned into compost.

Plastic bags can be used again and again until they break.

Even apparently useless things needn't be thrown away. Aluminum, steel, glass and plastic can all be melted down and used over and over again. Waste paper can be turned back into new paper.

Collecting old material and making it into new material is known as recycling. It saves space in landfills and saves energy too.

Making a can from recycled aluminum saves enough energy to power a television for three hours.

Every bottle made from recycled glass saves enough energy to light a room for four hours.

And for each foot-high stack of paper that's recycled, a ten-foot tall tree is saved.

It's surprising what plastic bottles can be recycled into...

5 bottles = stuffing for 1 ski jacket

1,000 bottles = 1 park bench

Chapter 8

How recycling works

Governments around the world are beginning to take recycling seriously. They're building recycling facilities in every town and even fining people who don't use them.

Now there are warehouses where hi-tech equipment sorts everything to be recycled.

1. Recycling is emptied into a large cylinder with holes.

6. Blasts of air separate the plastic from the glass.

5. Electric currents pull out the aluminum cans.

7. Workers check any items left over.

2. Bottles, cans and jars spin out, leaving the paper behind.

3. The bottles, cans and jars travel along a conveyor belt.

4. Magnets attract the steel cans.

8. The paper, plastic, steel, aluminum and glass are packed in bales and sent to be recycled.

Recycling paper

1. Paper is separated by quality.

Office paper

Newspaper

Cardboard

2. Machines soak and clean the paper. Paperclips, staples and tape are removed.

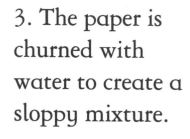

3. The paper is churned with water to create a sloppy mixture.

58

4. Big rollers squeeze the water out of the mixture.

5. Once dry, the paper is rolled up and stored.

6. The paper roll is made into anything from egg cartons to gift wrap.

Paper can be recycled four times before it becomes too mushy to use again.

Recycling plastic

1. The plastic is washed.

2. It's chopped into flakes.

3. The flakes are dumped into a tank of water and separated into different types.

Some types float...

others sink.

4. The different flakes are dried, then heated until they melt.

5. Melted plastic is shaped into long strands.

6. The strands are cooled in water, then chopped into little pellets.

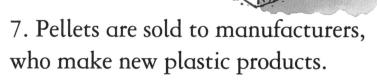

7. Pellets are sold to manufacturers, who make new plastic products.

61

Recycling cans

1. Shred the cans

2. Melt the metal

3. Cool into solid bars

4. Send the bars to a can factory

Recycling glass

1. Sort bottles by color

2. Clean and crush them

3. Melt the crushed glass

4. Make more bottles

If you look inside a garbage can, you'll see that over four fifths could be recycled or turned into compost.

paper (23%)

kitchen and garden waste (37%)

plastic (9%)

glass (8%)

metals (6%)

the rest (17%)

And if garbage isn't recycled? It might take over the world.

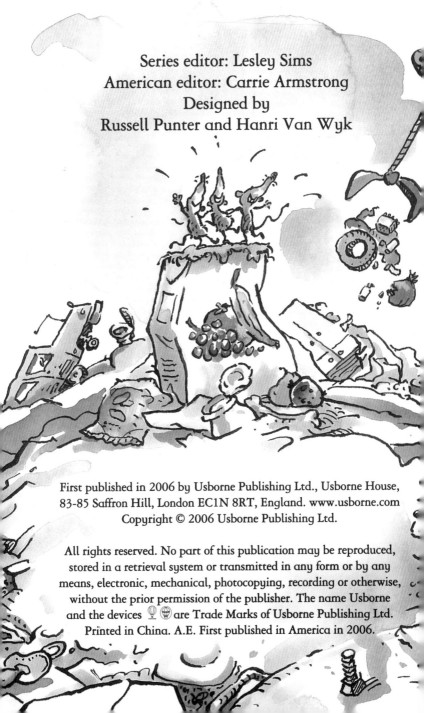

Series editor: Lesley Sims
American editor: Carrie Armstrong
Designed by
Russell Punter and Hanri Van Wyk